DUCK TO THE RESCUE

John Himmelman

Henry Holt and Company

New York

Henry Holt and Company, LLC
Publishers since 1866
175 Fifth Avenue
New York, New York 10010
mackids.com

Library of Congress Cataloging-in-Publication Data
Himmelman, John, author, illustrator.
Duck to the rescue / John Himmelman. — First edition.
pages   cm
Summary: When something goes wrong on the farm, Ernie the duck is determined to help out,
but no matter how hard he tries, nothing goes quite as he plans.
ISBN 978-0-8050-9485-5 (hardcover)
[1. Ducks—Fiction. 2. Farm life—Fiction. 3. Humorous stories.] I. Title.
PZ7.H5686Du 2013   [E]—dc23   2012027681

Henry Holt books may be purchased for business or promotional use. For information on bulk
purchases, please contact Macmillan Corporate and Premium Sales Department at
(800) 221-7945 x5442 or by e-mail at specialmarkets@macmillan.com.

First Edition—2014
The artist used black Prismacolor pencils and watercolors to create the illustrations for this book.
Printed in China by Toppan Leefung Printing Ltd., Dongguan City, Guangdong Province.

1 3 5 7 9 10 8 6 4 2

For Groucho and Duncan

On Monday, Farmer Greenstalk said, "I wish I had time to get the pumpkins to the market."

Duck to the rescue!

"I guess we can turn them into pumpkin pie," said the farmer.

On Tuesday, the little calf climbed too high in the barn.

Duck to the rescue!

"Moo," said the calf.

On Wednesday, the chickens needed a break from watching their chicks.

Duck to the rescue!

"Cluck cluck cluck," said the chickens.

On Thursday, the lights went out. Emily was afraid of the dark.

Duck to the rescue!

"Thanks, Ernie," said Emily.

On Friday, the scarecrow fell down.

Duck to the rescue!

"It's probably better to leave that job to a real scarecrow," said Mrs. Greenstalk.

On Saturday, Jeffrey needed another player for his soccer team.

Duck to the rescue!

"Maybe soccer isn't for you," said Jeffrey.

On Sunday, the little lamb "lost" his two cupcakes.

Duck to the rescue!!!